# The Pigeon Wants a Puppy!

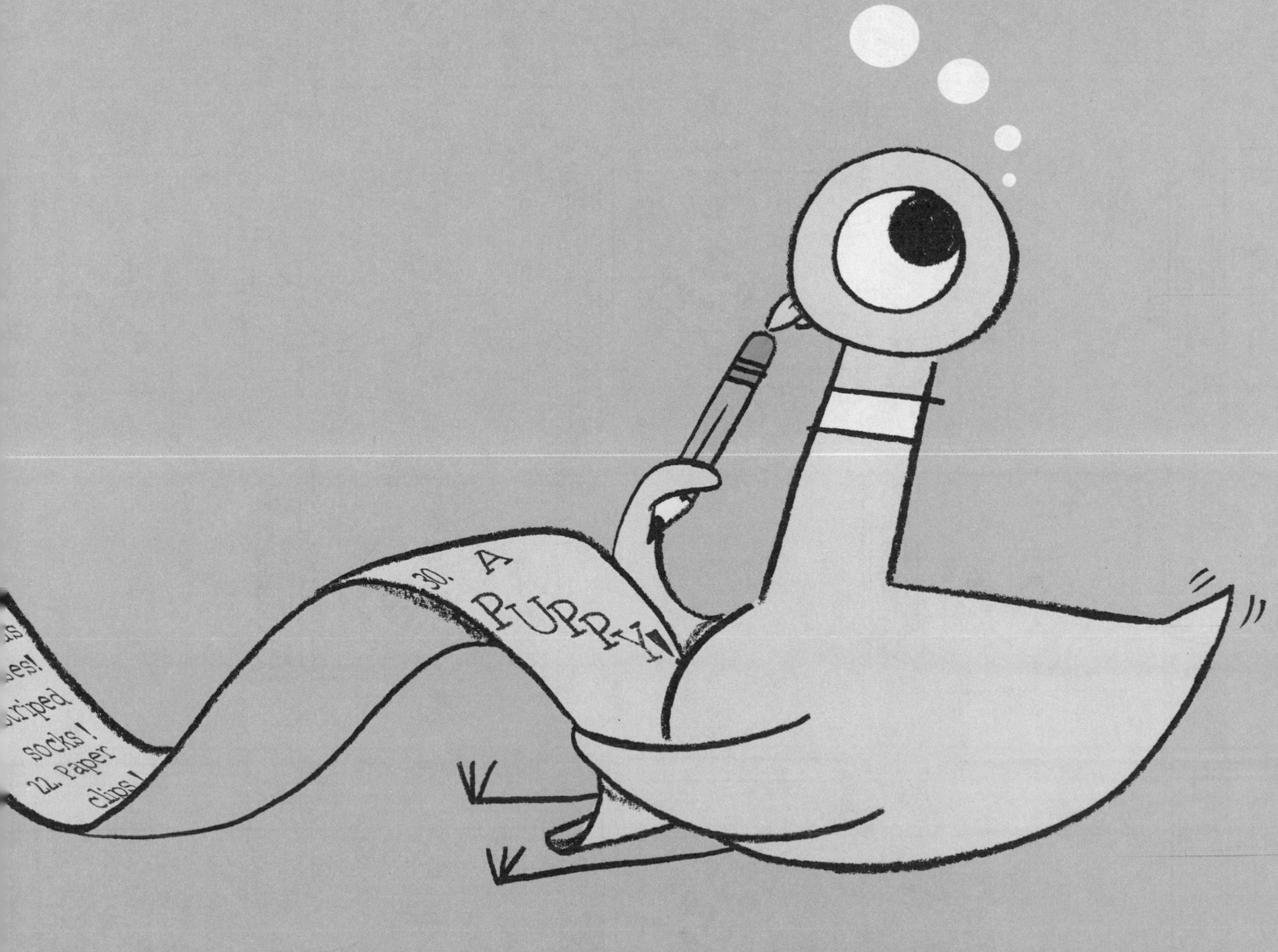

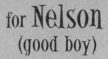

for **Nelson**
(good boy)

ISBN-13: 978-0-545-15770-4
ISBN-10: 0-545-15770-6

Text and illustrations copyright © 2008 by Mo Willems. All rights reserved. Published by Scholastic Inc., 557 Broadway, New York, NY 10012, by arrangement with Hyperion Books for Children, an imprint of Disney Book Group, LLC. SCHOLASTIC and associated logos are trademarks and/or registered trademarks of Scholastic Inc.

12 11 10 9 8 7 6 5 4 3 2 1                         9 10 11 12 13 14/0

Printed in the U.S.A.                                               40

First Scholastic printing, April 2009

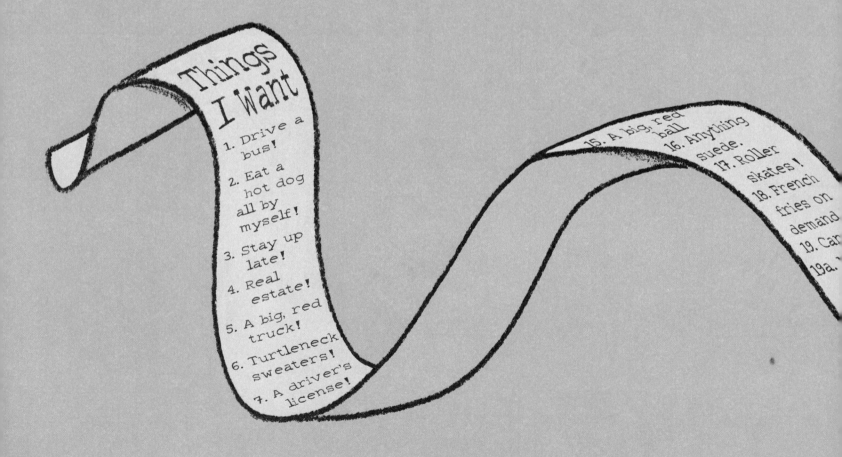

# The Pigeon Wants a Puppy!

words and pictures by mo willems

SCHOLASTIC INC.
New York  Toronto  London  Auckland  Sydney
Mexico City  New Delhi  Hong Kong  Buenos Aires

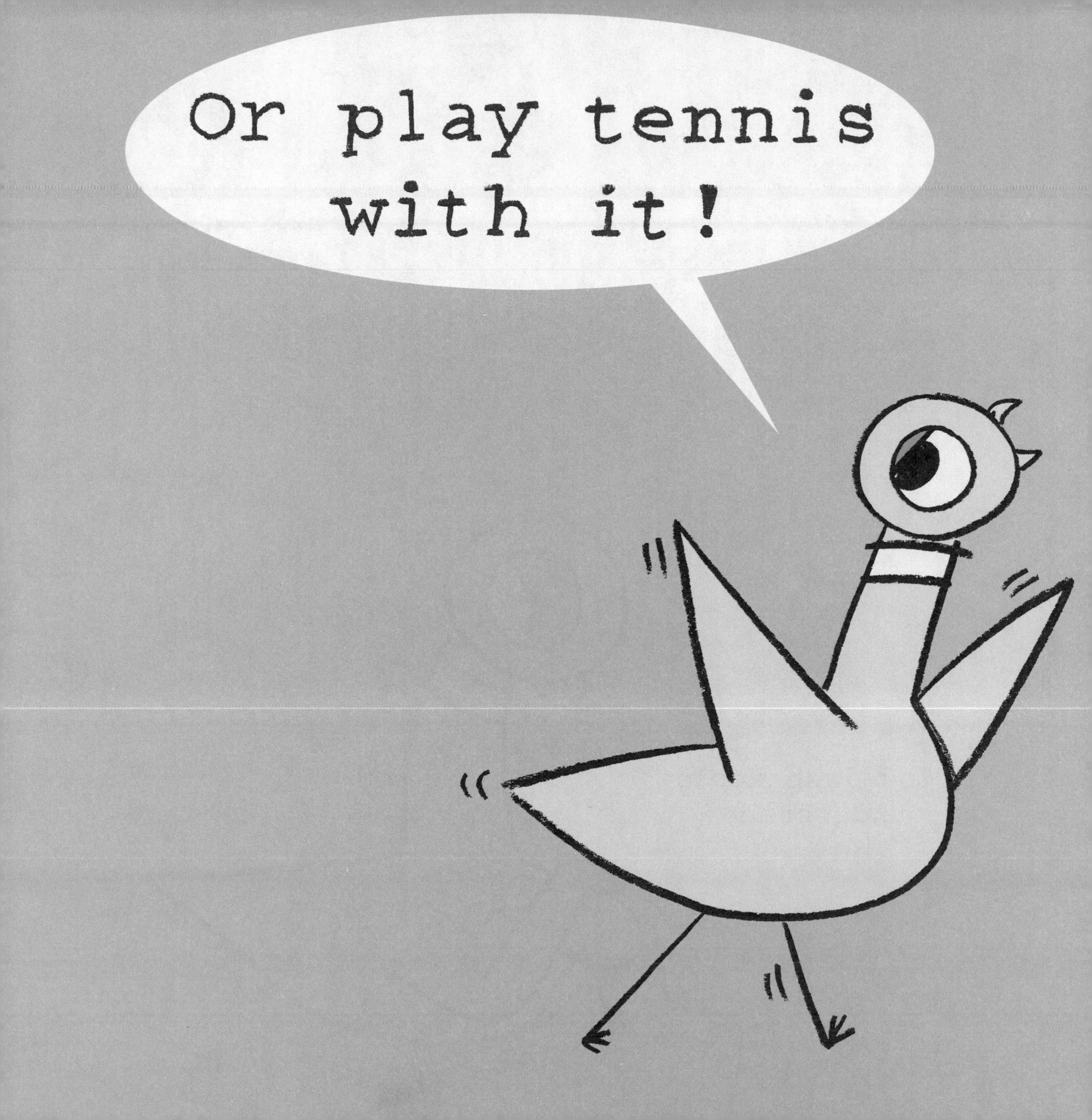
Or play tennis with it!

# I WANT A PUPPY! RIGHT HERE! RIGHT NOW!

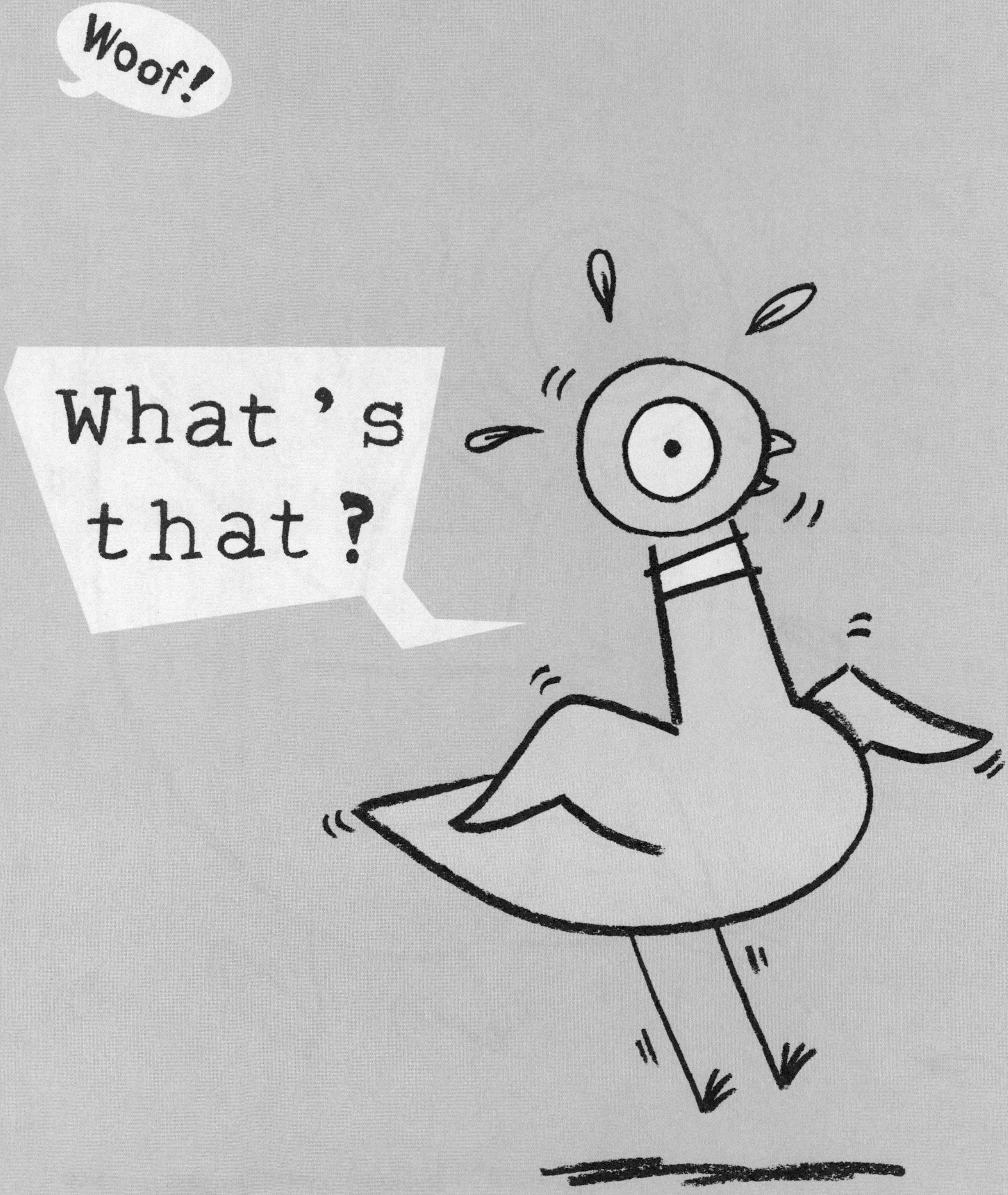
Woof!
What's that?

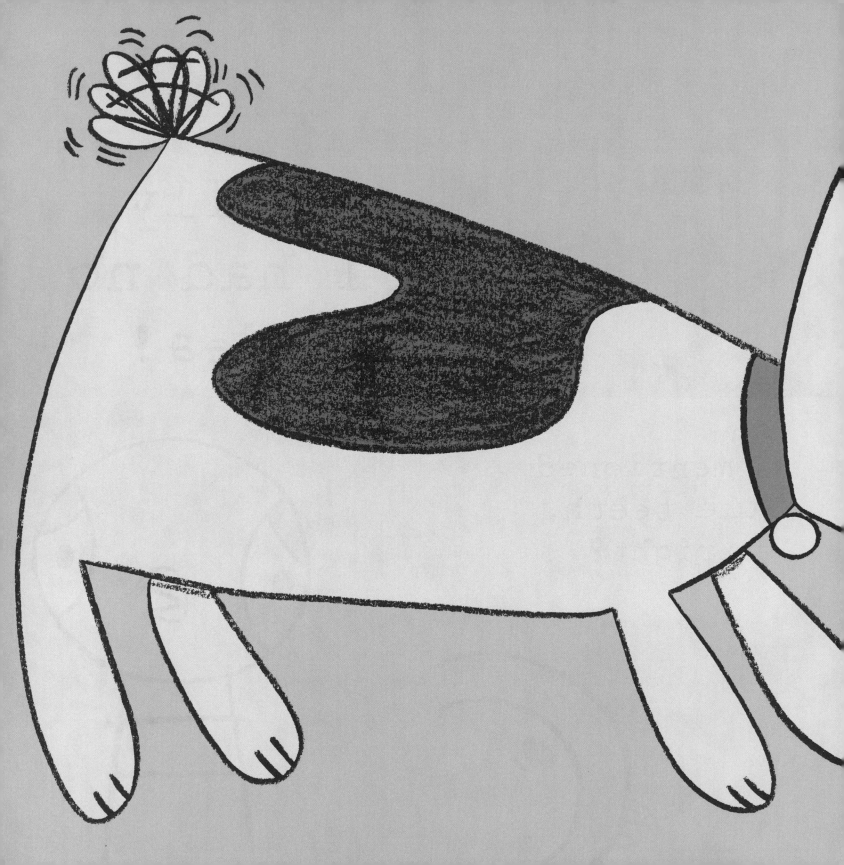